TOM JONES

KT-116-785

" QUOTE UNQUOTE "

TOM JONES

" QUOTE UNQUOTE "

Roger St. Pierre

PARRAGON

ACKNOWLEDGEMENTS

To Maureen O'Grady for all her painstaking work in researching this book.

The author and the publisher acknowledge the following references, where many of the quotes can be found:
Music Now, Billboard, Top Pops, Music Week, Oh Boy!, Daily Mirror, the *Sun, Decca records, NME Book of Rock*
(Salamander, 1973), *The Rock Handbook* (Salamander, 1971), *Daily Mail Book of Gold Discs* (Daily Mail Publications),
Tom Jones – A Biography by Stafford Hildred and David Gritten, *Tom Jones – The Boy From Nowhere* by Colin McFarlane

---

PICTURE CREDITS

Retna: © Beth Gwinn back cover; © Neal Preston 6, 10, 15, 40, 79; © Jay Blakesburg 8; © King Collection 18, 43; © Mark Sennet 48, 54, 60; Rob Brown, Onyx 52; © E. I. Camp 77; **London International Features:** front cover, 9, 16, 19, 20, 22, 26, 27, 28, 30, 31, 32, 34, 36, 38, 39, 42, 46, 57, 58, 65; © Phil Loftus 12; © Ron Wolfson 42, 66; © Maureen Donaldson 44; © Gouert De Roos 45, 61; © Gregg de Guire 49; © Topline-West Light 50; © Downie 63; © Julian Barton 64; © David Fisher 69, 73, 74, 75;© Kristin Callahan 76

Every effort has been made to trace the copyright holders and we apologize in advance for any unintentional omissions. We would be pleased to insert the appropriate acknowledgement in any subsequent edition of this publication.

First published in Great Britain in 1996 by
Parragon Book Service Ltd
Unit 13–17
Avonbridge Trading Estate
Atlantic Road
Avonmouth
Bristol BS11 9QD

Copyright © Parragon Book Service Ltd 1996

All rights reserved. No part of this publication may be reproduced, stored in a retrieval system or transmitted, in any form or by any means, electronic or mechanical including photocopying, recording or by any information storage and retrieval system, without the prior permission of the copyright holder.

ISBN: 0-7525-1696-5

Produced by Haldane Mason, London

Editor: Paul Barnett
Design: Digital Artworks Partnership Ltd
Picture Research: Charles Dixon-Spain

Printed in Italy

CONTENTS

HOW GREEN WAS HIS VALLEY? 6

THE DREAM BEGINS .16

IT WAS UNUSUAL 28

AMERICA CALLING 40

THE VEGAS HIGH ROLLER 54

IN THE GROOVE 66

HOW GREEN WAS HIS VALLEY?

'My parents were very important to me. I don't look back on my childhood and think of any bad times. My mother often gave me slaps but to me it was needed . . . If I got the hell knocked out of me it was deserved. When you've lived the life of Laura Street you don't forget it.'

FACING PAGE: *The man from the valleys, who still possesses a great deal of the sexual charisma which first brought him to the notice of his adoring public.*

IF YOU LOOK in the list of the 100 all-time bestselling recording stars, you will not find Tom Jones there. In fact, his hit-making period spanned less than half a decade, and that was a quarter of a century ago. But when at the end of 1995 the British tabloids splashed stories of three-in-a-bed sex romps across their front pages, they were writing about not some old, long-forgotten has-been but a man who still counts his active fans – nearly all of them women – in the millions.

Though now a grandfather, the boyo from the Welsh valleys remains one of the great show-business icons, an enduring sex symbol whose every new exploit helps sell newspapers by the bundle and whose shows still sell out regularly. True, his best records – notably the three mega-hits, 'It's Not Unusual', 'Delilah' and 'The Green, Green Grass of Home' – remain classics that are still played regularly on oldies shows around the world, but, just like Elvis Presley – the superstar with whom he has most often been compared – Tom has also recorded an awful lot of rubbish.

However, he has rarely given a poor show. Long before the likes of Rick Wakeman and Pink Floyd, Tom and his manager Gordon Mills realized that spectacle was the name of the game; while he has often been accused of being extraordinarily mean in his business dealings and private relationships, he has never been stingy with his audience – giving them huge orchestras, massed singers, elaborate sets and big-name support acts as the extravagant showcase for his magically rich voice and those outrageously overt

RIGHT: On stage showing both the sartorial flare and crooning sensibility which has made Tom so popular all over the world.

RIGHT: Tom and Freda Woodward were proud that their son had made the big time — even if he changed his name to do it.

stage moves. No wonder Las Vegas has loved him!

In Wales the name Jones is so commonplace that to ease identification a man's occupation is usually appended — 'Jones the Post', 'Jones the Driver', and so on. In Tom Jones's case it presumably should be 'Jones the Sex'. Not that 'Jones' was actually his original name, nor even the stage name with which he first strove for stardom. Born in Pontypridd on June 7, 1940, he was named Thomas John Woodward, after his father. Although Thomas Sr was a miner, Tom himself never in fact worked down the pits, despite the claims of some early biographies.

Tom's parents said that even as a six-month-old baby their son was already making musical notes, and certainly he began singing at a very youthful age. His mother, Freda, once recalled: 'From the earliest days I could see the talent there. When he was only two-and-a-half he was like a professional singer. He would pull our drape curtains across, get behind them and say: "Mum, call me out to sing now."'

Uncle George, himself no mean singer, gave the toddler his first lesson in stage technique: 'Sing to the people's

'When I was able to stand I was already able to sing. When mum took me to the corner shop I'd stand on an orange box and sing to the people who came in. At school I'd do the same thing — any chance I'd get I would sing.'

> '*I always wanted to be a singer since I was a child. In Wales everybody sings because there is a lot of opportunity to sing . . . people used to say that I had a good voice so I was always encouraged to sing.*'

faces — let them see what you are singing about.' And Brother Edwin remembered years later: 'He'd be taken into pubs and put up on a chair to sing. He loved all the attention.'

Tom's first earnings as a singer were found in Tom Marney's little post-office-cum-general-store in Wood Street: his mother told *Music Now!* that after one impromptu performance the shopkeeper urged his customers, 'Come on, give the lad a few coppers.'

At Treforest Primary School, Tom stood up in front of his class and sang 'Ghost Riders in the Sky'. 'He couldn't have been much older than five or six at the time,' according to school chum Brian Blackler. One teacher even told

RIGHT: Mean and moody — Tom grew up as a quick tempered street-fighter, though his voice soon became more important than his fists.

Tom off for drowning out the rest of the school choir when they sang the Welsh national song, 'Men of Harlech', in assembly. Another was amazed that a child from the Welsh valleys could sound so much like a black American gospel performer when singing the Lord's Prayer.

Money did not come easily to mining families and life in the Woodwards' terraced family home at 44 Laura Street was frugal. Tom was certainly streetwise from an early age and soon earned a reputation as a bit of a tearaway. When it came to school, though, he was something of a wastrel, preferring to listen to the latest hits on Radio Luxembourg or Jack Jackson's groundbreaking pop show on the BBC's Light Programme rather than get on with his schoolwork. He was frequently marked 'absent' in the register at Treforest Secondary School, invoking his parents' ire.

He had been just 11 when he met his first love. Melinda (Linda) Trenchard, who lived just round the corner at 3 Cliff Terrace, Treforest, would become his long-term wife, although she was far from the only woman in his life. Soon after meeting her, though, he fell ill from tuberculosis, which at that time was a major scourge, particularly in working-class communities. It laid him up in bed for a year, but he certainly did not waste away; on the contrary, the good food and the care he received during his convalescence transformed him from the short, thin boy Linda had first seen into a tall, chubby, robust teenager. The brown hair of his childhood had darkened to black: 'When we met up again after he went back to school', she later told *Top of the Pops* magazine, 'I didn't recognize him at first, but I was immediately attracted to him again.'

The illness had certainly not damaged Tom's emerging libido. Although his

---

'As a kid, I watched Larry Parks portray Al Jolson on film and I decided there was something special about using those mechanisms of dropping to one knee, the outstretched arm, the constant movement — getting across to the audience. I thought: "I want to be like that."'

feelings towards Linda might have been a matter of love at first sight, he still had an eye for other girls. As a local journalist who grew up with him recalled: 'He got a reputation as . . . a tearaway but the girls were attracted by that rebel thing. I can remember him at the local swimming baths, swaggering around wearing white trunks with his comb always stuck inside them. He was always posing and preening himself – but it worked, the girls loved him.'

Male chauvinism was almost a religion in the South Wales communities of that time – and Tom was certainly a follower of the faith. While he enjoyed Linda's company, he demanded plenty of time off to run around with his mates, one of whom was Dai Perry, later his bodyguard for a short period. 'We were like brothers, me and Tom,' said Dai. 'We used to play together, fight together and drink together. We got served in pubs from when we were 13 or 14. It was a hard area, still is, but in those days the fights were fair. There were no knives or any of that nonsense. Tom was tough – he could look after himself.'

Tom was a big lad, and indeed tough – maybe not exactly a bully but always with a reputation as a bit of a lout with a

LEFT: Tom Jones with bubbly Glaswegian singer Lulu, another of the stars who helped Britain dominate Sixties pop music.

quick temper and a thirst not just for beer but for a punch-up — though, in that neck of the woods, head-butting was the preferred mode of attack. As the neighbours remarked, Tom 'didn't half fancy himself', and there was no shortage of local yobbos set on taking him down a peg or two. And he didn't always come out the better for wear. Years afterwards, remembering once having been thrown through the plate-glass window of his local fish-and-chip shop, he commented. 'I hate my horrible nose. It's been worked over, bent sideways and patched up more than any other part of me. It got broken so many times in punch-ups that I can't remember which particular incident made it this shape!'

It was the era of the Teddy Boys, rebels without a cause who liked to sport their hair long, greased and worked into an outrageous quiff. They wore drape jackets that came down to their knees, bootlace ties, 'drainpipe' trousers so tight they had to peel them off, and chunky crepe-soled 'brothel creeper' shoes. Tom was most decidedly a Ted but, when the style metamorphosed and being a Rocker was more fashionable, he simply swapped his velvet collar for black leather and became a Rocker.

However, responsibility soon came knocking at his door. Linda, still only 15 years old, discovered she was pregnant; Tom, only 16 himself, was soon to become a father. Teenage pregnancies were hardly unknown in the close-knit Welsh mining communities of that time. Indeed, a much-told joke ran: 'I hear the Evans girl is getting married. When's the baby due?' 'Oh, no, she's not pregnant. It's a posh wedding, look you!' Nevertheless, for Linda and Tom the experience was highly traumatic. Aside from their youth, the fact that Linda was Roman Catholic and Tom a Protestant did not help. Tom later recalled the agony: 'They were all sitting in our bloody house, discussing what was going to happen to us and our unborn baby. There was my mother and father and Linda's parents and the two of us were sitting in the corner, holding hands and not saying anything.'

He also remembered his father's supportive stance: 'He suddenly burst out: "Hey, we're talking about them as if they are not here and we are trying to decide their lives for them. Let's hear from them. What do you want to do, Tom?" I said we wanted to get married and for Linda to have the baby and he stood up against the rest of them and said, "Go ahead." And later, when various of our relatives argued against the marriage, saying we were too young, he stood firm against them.'

In fact, the pair had to wait until Linda was legally of age before they were

---

'I never said anything about Linda to my mates — she was always special you see. The boys used to ask "Have you given her one yet?" and I always used to say "No!" I was very protective about her. I used to chat about sex but I could never have chatted about my sweetheart.'

---

able to get married. The knot was tied at the Pontypridd Registry Office on March 2, 1957, and the teenage couple moved into the basement of Linda's mother's house. Son Mark — who many years later was to become his father's manager — was born on April 11 in Cardiff Maternity Hospital.

Not long out of school and with a young family to support, Tom had to knuckle down to a job. His first employment, as an apprentice glove-maker, earned him £2 a week, and he hated it. Then he worked in a paper mill for a similar pittance, getting a rise only when, after a year, he went to the boss and said: 'I think I can run the machine. I can do a man's job and I need to earn a man's money.'

Tom was just 17 at the time, and the promotion didn't please everyone: 'Some of the older workers saw me as a young upstart and they'd try to screw me up at work by interfering with the settings of the machine. One guy even tried to provoke me into hitting him so I would be sacked.' But by no means everyone was against him. He fondly recalls workmate Billy Larcombe encouraging him: 'He was an old chap and one day when I was working these long hours he said to me: "What are you doing here?" I replied that I was trying to make a bloody living just like him, and he then said: "Yeah, but I'm an old man. I've been in the army, been all over the world. I've done the best I could with my life. But I've heard you sing. You've got a great voice and you should make the best of it. When

ABOVE: Tom is a born poser, but in front of the camera he has seldom allowed himself to be caught in an unguarded moment.

'A lot of my friends got married when they were 16 or 17. They started work at 15, many of them going down the mines. Once you are working you think you are a man. You want to go drinking with the boys. You think you are an adult and being married is part of it, it's proving that you are capable.'

you see your chance – go for it. There are fellows working round here who could have been great soccer players, rugby stars or whatever, but they let the opportunity slip them by. Don't go doing the same. Have a crack – you can always come back here later if it doesn't work out.'"

'When Mark was born I didn't have two pennies to rub together. I was excited but my first thought was whether I'd be able to support him and do him justice. I was working nights at the paper mill and couldn't afford to take the shift off. As Linda was leaving in the ambulance, I was setting off for work on my bike.'

THE DREAM BEGINS

'I actually started as drummer in a group, but that was strictly amateur stuff. I bought a guitar when I was 15 and sang at parties and in clubs, but I was very limited on my own. Once I had a taste of singing with a band I realized that it was what I was looking for.'

FACING PAGE: Here Tom plays the sophisticated crooner — a persona he shed as the Sixties progressed.

YOUNG TOM WOODWARD wanted his life to mean something more than the daily grind of a steady job. Taking Billy Larcombe's advice to heart, as soon as he was able to he turned his innate singing talent into an earner of ready cash. And cash it was – he became part of the black economy, he quit his day job at the mill and became what contemporaries like local pop music critic Gerry Greenberg, of the *Pontypridd Observer*, described as 'a layabout who didn't like working'. Added Gerry: 'By the time I met him, in 1961, he had changed his name to Tommy Scott and

BELOW: Not just another rocker, but a star in the making, though here the sharp style has still to emerge.

was fronting a local band called the Senators. You would often see him idling the day away on street corners, always clad in the obligatory T-shirt, leather jacket, turned-up jeans and winklepicker shoes. He looked like a Welsh model for the Fonz.'

As Stafford Hildred and David Gritten remarked in their excellent book *Tom Jones – A Biography*, Tom's regular chore was a Tuesday-morning stroll along Taff Street to the dole office to draw his unemployment benefit. But nobody could have claimed that Tom was shy of work once he got on stage of an evening.

He had joined the Senators as replacement for vocalist Tommy Redman, who unfortunately felt the call of the gaming table more than that of the stage. Having had to cover three nights in a row for their absent singer, the group's bass guitarist and main organizer, Vernon Hopkins, made a snap decision, raced out of the YMCA and down the road to the White Hart, at the other end of the High Street, where he knew Tom would be drinking with his mates. Vernon promised to smuggle a crate of beer in through the back door of the teetotal YMCA for Tom to sup between songs, and so the singer joined the Senators on

RIGHT: Tom, back in the green, green valleys of his homeland. Though he has lived away for years, he has always been proud of his Welsh origins.

stage for what proved to be a momentous evening.

Within days a meeting was called at Vernon's house. Later Vernon reminisced: 'My sister brought us in sandwiches, biscuits and tea. Both Tom Woodward and Tom Pittman – Tommy Redman's real name – were there. We all had our say and took a vote, and that's how we came to make the change of singers permanent.'

For Tom Woodward, it also meant a name change. Vernon again: 'We decided he should have a new name if he was joining the group. I popped into a phone box and scanned through the directory. I fancied something beginning with "S", saw the name Scott and thought: "Tommy Scott and the Senators – that sounds magic."'

It was the era of Beatlemania and the Merseybeat boom. Besides the Fab Four, other Liverpool acts like Billy J. Kramer & the Dakotas, the Fourmost, Gerry & the Pacemakers, Cilla Black and – from nearby Manchester – the Searchers and the Hollies were starting to set the national charts alight and to draw attention on the other side of the Atlantic. Meanwhile, in London, the emergent R&B boom was throwing up such

'The working men's clubs had not seen electric guitars before and wondered what was happening. But when we got on stage they wouldn't let us off. We were doing rock'n'roll in the ballrooms but when we worked the clubs we gave them big strong ballads which I knew they'd enjoy.'

LEFT: All for one and one for all, the Senators arrived in London as a fully integrated group. Within months Tom Jones (right) had been catapulted to stardom and their name had been changed to the Squires — the other lads had become merely a backing band for Tom.

'rebels' as the Rolling Stones and the Pretty Things, to the despair of any parents with teenage kids.

It was also the time of the Mods, with their college-boy haircuts, natty suits and penchant for popping pills. Down in South Wales, however, the Senators were more like a throwback to the rock'n'roll Fifties: 'People in our home town would say, "For God's sake get to London and show the English what it's all about". Like me, they loved what people like Jerry Lee Lewis, Little Richard and Chuck Berry had been doing for close on a decade,' says Tom.

When Jerry Lee Lewis and the Big Bopper played the Sophia Gardens, Cardiff, Tom was waiting afterwards at the stage door. The stars rushed out and jumped into a limo, but Tom hailed a cab and yelled the immortal cliché 'Follow that car!' He jumped out at some traffic lights and grabbed the opportunity to get the autographs of his heroes.

Tom was in earnest in his singing – taking it seriously enough that he embarked on lessons with a local music teacher to improve his breathing techniques: 'There were a lot of people who had faith in me, who gave me confidence. My family, of course, and

friends, too, as well as people in the clubs,' he remembers.

At home, the Senators' reputation was big enough for them to blow many a visiting big-name star off the stage – but how would the nation at large react? To find out, they needed a bit of outside help. It came from two young Welsh-based songwriters who likewise had a broader vision of their own future.

One of them, Raymond Godfrey, recounts: 'Back in 1962, John Glastonbury and I were partners trying to get London music publishers to take up our songs. We really wanted to make the big time. On one of our forays up to town we were told we should find a band to put our material on to a demo disc, so the next day we went to a dance hall in Caerphilly to see three groups who were performing there. We were very impressed with Tommy Scott and the Senators – especially with Tom's voice. When they came off stage, we introduced ourselves and asked if they'd be interested in cutting a demo for us. Right from the off, though, it was Tom we were really interested in, and it was not long before we had extended our role to being the act's managers.'

RIGHT: *The big voice from the valleys, Tom Jones built his following on raw sex appeal.*

Discipline was certainly not the group's strongest suit and it took several abortive rehearsals – the lads arriving late or not at all – before the first usable demo was finally recorded on a portable tape deck, the venue being the Pontypridd YMCA toilets because, according to the Senators' then rhythm guitarist, Keith Davies, 'that's where the acoustics were best'.

The results were passable, but getting a deal wasn't going to be easy. It was a boom time for the music industry, with record sales reaching unprecedented heights, but the carpets of London's big companies were being worn threadbare by aspiring performers from all over the country. There was simply too much material on offer for any A&R man to be able to audition it all. It was a feat of sheer dogged perseverance even to get an appointment, and if you landed a contract, well, that was a near miracle. Eventually, though, 'Myron and Byron' – as Tom had dubbed the two managers – succeeded in interesting Joe Meek, a mercurial independent producer who had just had a 1962 Number One with the Tornadoes' instrumental 'Telstar'.

According to *Record Mirror*'s Peter Kent, 'Meek was a bullying, hot-tempered and unpredictable character prone to constant mood swings. Not afraid of violence, he eventually turned it on himself by committing suicide.' Appointments with him would be broken; meetings were chaotic, being plagued by mood-changes, tantrums and constant flying-off at tangents. What's more, in those days before the existence of

---

'The two guys who were managing me used to say that I sang like Joe Williams. I'd say: "He's a jazz singer, how can I sound like him?" But they meant that the way I projected my voice was like him.'

M4 motorway and the Severn Bridge, South Wales was a tedious six- or seven-hour drive away from Meek's North London base, making the trip a wearisome ordeal – especially when, as usually happened, the business of the day went uncompleted.

By early 1963 seven tracks had finally been laid down and, with 'Lonely

Joe', a song written by the then-popular Avons, as the A-side and the Godfrey/Glastonbury composition 'I Was a Fool' scheduled for the flipside, the imminent appearance of a single – leased by Meek to one of the majors – was promised.

It was a promise that was never kept: 'He told us that Decca had picked up the record and that it would be coming out, but each time the date came and went with a different excuse,' says Raymond Godfrey. 'He'd tell us the release had been put back because someone else had a similar record out, because the timing wasn't right or some other, often implausible reason. He strung us along for nine totally frustrating months. Eventually it became almost impossible even to get him on the phone, so one morning we knocked on his door at 10a.m., after

driving through the night, and insisted on seeing him there and then. He tried to tell us he was too busy but we wouldn't go away, and insisted that things had to be sorted out there and then. He flew into a rage, said he'd had enough and wanted out, so we took our contract back and drove home to Wales to tell the boys.'

So it was back to square one. Tom himself had never been overimpressed with Myron and Byron's efficacy as deal-makers, and it was he who broke the impasse: 'One of them had been up in London for a week and we hadn't heard a thing, so I went looking for him. I banged on the door of his hotel room and who should come out of the room next door but Jimmy Savile. We had a chat and he gave me some good advice. Myron – or was it Byron? – had been staying next door to this so-powerful disc jockey for a week and hadn't even made contact. I couldn't believe it. Jimmy was real nice and told me I should come and see him next day. I recorded four songs, he gave the demo tape to the people at Decca, and that was that.'

Jimmy himself remarked: 'If it hadn't been me, it would have been someone else.' But Tom has never forgotten that

---

'Eddie Brown, a local bookmaker, used to show off his E-type Jaguar. I remember saying, "One day I'll have a dozen of them"'

---

good turn. Years later, Jimmy hosted a popular television series called *Jim'll Fix It* in which he made viewers' dreams come true. As Colin Macfarlane put it in his excellent biography *Tom Jones — The Boy from Nowhere*, 'Perhaps this was Jimmy's first fix-it.' Decca staff A&R man Peter Sullivan promised Tom a contract.

But then the trail went cold again. This was the cue for Gordon Mills, the man destined to play the biggest role of all in turning Tom Woodward, Welsh miner's son, into Tom Jones, international superstar.

Gordon was another product of the valleys, having grown up in Tonypandy, where he started his working life as a bus conductor. A fine musician, in the late Fifties he finished runner-up in the British Harmonica Championships, held in the grandiose setting of London's Royal Albert Hall, an appearance which led to a successful audition with the then-popular Morton Frazer Harmonica Gang variety act. Not long afterwards Gordon moved on to a group called the Viscounts, with which he enjoyed a few minor hits as lead singer. But it was the business side of the music industry which exerted the most appeal for him. A born wheeler-dealer who could think big and keep his feet firmly on the ground at the same time, Gordon decided that management was where his fortune lay.

Gordon had heard talk from an old schoolfriend, Gordon Jones, of how good Tommy Scott was, and on a visit to his parents he and his wife Jo — then expecting their first child — decided to check out the Senators' act. A singer friend named Johnny Bennett took them to the Lewis Merthyr Club, in Porth, one Sunday morning: 'I pointed Tom out, and Gordon said: "Not that scruffy bastard, surely?" Tom was in leather jacket and jeans. I told Gordon he wouldn't dress like that when he went on stage to perform, and persuaded Gordon we should see the Senators' show that evening at the Top Hat Club, in Cwmtillery. They weren't impressed by Gordon's credentials and, as he wasn't a member, we had to stand at the back to watch the show.'

Gordon, though, was certainly impressed by Tom. When asked what her husband thought, Jo Mills responded: 'If Gordon hadn't liked the show he would have been straight out of the door after the first song.' She added: 'For my part, I was absolutely stunned by Tom's performance. It was an amazing experience.

LEFT: Under the tutelage of the incredibly astute Gordon Mills, Tom developed a carefully balanced image, which combined overt sexiness with thoughtfulness and sensitivity.

RIGHT: Frilly shirt and fuzzy hair-do — just one stage in the development of Tom's ever-evolving persona.

He was just a remarkable raw talent. On the way back to London, Gordon suddenly pulled into the side of the road, turned to me and said: "I've just got to do something with that guy." And it was there and then that he [finally] decided to get into management.'

'It happened like I thought it would happen. I knew that one day somebody would see my talent and say: "I'm going to take you to London and get a hit for you" – and that is exactly what happened.'

Gordon Mills himself said of that night: 'As soon as I saw Tom I knew he had what it takes to get right to the top. The first few bars convinced me that here was a voice which could make him the best singer in the world.'

IT WAS UNUSUAL

'It was the age of outrage. They wanted you to be different. I had a Tony Curtis haircut instead of a Mick Jagger haircut. It was strange — they said I was too masculine.'

JUST AS IT USED TO BE the case that all roads led to Rome, for aspiring young pop stars in the Swinging Sixties they all led to London. That's where Gordon Mills was convinced that Tommy Scott and the Senators should head — and, to make it happen, he was prepared to invest most of the royalties which he had earned from writing the Johnny Kidd and the Pirates hit 'I'll Never Get Over You'.

He had already persuaded Tom that he, Gordon, should take over as the singer's manager. As Raymond Godfrey remembered it: 'Tom told us that he had received this offer from Gordon Mills, who had even said Tom could stay at his flat if he moved to London. We had a valid management contract but we could see that Tom had made his mind up and, in any event, we didn't want to hold him back, so we agreed to let him go, provided we had an ongoing five per cent override on his future earnings, and he agreed to that.' In the event, Gordon found the group accommodation in a grotty two-bedroomed flat in Ladbroke Grove, a rather seedy district of West London which, besides being a haunt of pop stars who had yet to make it, was a favoured beat for ladies of the night. He paid the boys £1 a day each.

Vernon Hopkins, who had been the mainstay of the group from the start, gave up his steady job as a printer in a newspaper works to make the move. Mickey Gee — who, unlike the rest, was not from the valleys but from Cardiff —

LEFT: *All in the very best taste! Tom has always savoured the trappings of stardom.*

quit his job as a beer-delivery man and came in as lead guitarist to replace original member Mike Roberts, who was not prepared to give up his relatively well-paid day job as a television cameraman. Chris Rees, at 17 the baby of the group, changed his name to Chris Slade and terminated his studies at Pontypridd Grammar School, much to the dismay of his parents. They were joined by rhythm guitarist Dave 'Dai' Cooper, who had replaced Keith Davies and at whose parents' hotel in Abercynon the group had regularly rehearsed.

Tom, of course, had to leave behind his wife and infant son. He also changed his stage name again, this time because there was already a Tommy Scott on the music scene. The choice of 'Jones' was not so much because of its Welshness but because of the movie *Tom Jones* (1963), which was a major box-office hit at the time. The group altered its name, too, from the Senators to the trendy-for-the-time Playboys.

The move came in June 1964, and two months later their first Decca release finally appeared: 'Chills and Fever', one of the songs from the Joe Meek sessions. Said Raymond Godfrey, who with that five-per-cent stake still had a financial interest in success, 'Peter Sullivan, who had signed Tom to Decca, really wanted to get something out on the market quickly, but we thought that record was awful. It was grossly overproduced, with lashings of piano and brass overdubs. It sounded more like the Hallé Orchestra than a pop group with a singer.'

Not surprisingly, this debut record flopped, leading to what was to be the

ABOVE: *We're looking good! Watching a rehearsal playback for one of those memorable Tom Jones TV shows. The worldwide audience ran into millions and Lew Grade made Tom one of TV's highest earners.*

blackest period of Tom's career, a time of considerable self-doubt. Making it on the London live-gig scene wasn't going to be easy. While a Liverpudlian, Glaswegian or even Irish accent was rather hip, being Welsh was decidedly untrendy, and the group's stage outfits did nothing to help. As Mickey Gee remembered it:

BELOW: TV shows like Ready, Steady, Go! in 1964 projected Tom to a teenage audience.

'We'd support the Rolling Stones and all those other hairy groups of the time at a club called Beat City, on Oxford Street, and Tom would come out with his skin-tight trousers and frilly shirts, while we'd be wearing matching Marks & Spencer shirts which Gordon had bought us and all had our hair dyed black to match Tom's. We were on a different planet from the other groups.' What's more, at 24 years old, Tom was already well past the sell-by date for most pop stars in that youth-obsessed era. Says Tom: 'We had lots of auditions, but most of the agents would say "too adult", "too old-fashioned" or "too rock'n'roll". Gordon thought they would snap us up, but we just weren't right for the club scene at that time.' As Stafford Hildred and David Gritten put it in *Tom Jones – A Biography*: 'This was an age of baby-faced, almost girlish-looking pop stars – Paul McCartney, long-haired Mick Jagger, Billy J. Kramer and Peter Noone of Herman's Hermits. Tom Jones, on the other hand, might have passed for a worker on a building site or a long-distance lorry driver. He was definitely nobody's idea of a fresh-faced star in this age of British pop.'

'It didn't help that we were living on the poverty line,' said Mickey Gee. 'For months I had to go on stage from the left so I could hide a big ironing mark I had made on my trousers. At that time, Tom was just one of us — we were young Welsh yobs living away from home in London and trying to get by on £1 a day. Generally we all got on well. Tom and I did have one or two fights, but next day we were too hungover to remember why. He liked to get drunk and he liked to pull a bird. He wasn't choosy, he'd pull anything. His favourite trick was to run out of restaurants without paying the bill. At first it was because we were so hard up, but later, even when we could afford to pay, he would rush out and we would all panic and follow him through the door as quickly as we could.'

Back home several members of the group had been in steady jobs and, with the extra tenner or so that a gig made for them, had been relatively well off, but in London times were so tight that on one occasion they found themselves with just half-a-crown left between them. Tom and another member of the band went out to spend the money on some sandwiches but were so hungry that they ate them all on the way back, telling their disbelieving colleagues that they had lost the money down a drainhole.

And the group had to change its name yet again — discovering that there was already another band called the Playboys. This time they became the Squires — not that it eventually mattered much, because gradually the truth dawned on everyone that the rest were in reality merely a backing group for Tom Jones.

'Things weren't working out. My wife had to go out to work back in Wales to support herself and my son and that upset me because I was brought up to believe that a man provides for his family . . . It was on my mind to go back home.'

Even as he was slowly emerging as the dominant member of the setup, everything was getting on top of Tom, so much so that he thought of giving up and even contemplated suicide. Discovered alone at the flat one day, sobbing his heart out, he confessed to Vernon that

RIGHT: Tom seeking inspiration from his piano-pumping hero. He discovered his massive 'Green, Green Grass of Home' hit on one such Jerry Lee Lewis album.

he'd come close to jumping under a tube train at Notting Hill underground station. Vernon later commented: 'I told him that we were all fed up as well but that we were in it together. We'd come this far. We had to stick it out because we'd surely get a break eventually. It took a lot of hard persuasion but eventually I talked him into staying.'

Tom remembers that Gordon Mills was very good to him at this difficult time: 'But he was feeling the pinch too because his wife Jo was pregnant again so she'd had to give up her modelling work. They had spent all their funds and were running up a considerable overdraft, so he really couldn't afford to give me the extra £5 I was asking for to send down to Linda.'

The apprenticeship looked as if it was going to be long and hard and full of frustrating delays and disappointments. However, when success came, it did so quite literally overnight.

The reason was a song titled 'It's Not Unusual', which Gordon had penned in partnership with successful songwriter Les Reed. By this time the Squires, like most groups on the scene, had taken to the late-to-bed late-to-rise routine (which has, indeed, been the standard format of Tom Jones's lifestyle ever since). Gordon arrived at the flat one noon and turfed them out from under the covers, saying he had booked a studio in Denmark Street — London's famed equivalent of Tin Pan Alley — for three o'clock that afternoon so that they could cut a demo of the new song to play to Sandie Shaw and her management, who been pressing him to come up with some material for her.

Dave Cooper and Vernon Hopkins, who were archetypal three-chord wonders, couldn't get a grip on the song at all, so it was recorded without them — Tom sang, drummer Chris Slade played tambourine and Mickey Gee played lead guitar plus some rhythm overdubs.

'We went into the George pub across the street for a drink after the session, which had taken all of 20 minutes to record, and I rounded on Gordon,' said Mickey Gee. 'I told him the song was perfect for Tom and that it was a potential big hit, maybe not a guaranteed one for us as it would be for Sandie, but one he should at least let us get out on record.'

Tom kept up the pressure over the following weeks, and eventually Gordon

conceded that, while he had to stick to his promises to give Sandie Shaw's management the first offer, if she were to turn the song down then Tom could have it. And, though the song would have fitted her style perfectly, Sandie Shaw did indeed say 'no'. Her loss proved Tom Jones's gain.

LEFT: Tom sings with the passion of a gospel artist — earning him the attention of black America and, at one stage, the prospect of a contract with Motown.

'It was like I'd spent years in the dark, then someone opened the door and threw a great ray of light on me.'

The rest of the Squires lost out, too. The near-debacle of the demo sessions had convinced Gordon Mills that Tom required professional session musicians as backing. From that moment onwards Tom Jones and the Squires ceased to be an 'all for one and one for all' outfit, and the lads became mere hired help.

Not that the new sessions, at Decca's studios in West Hampstead, went smoothly even after the musical deficiencies of the Squires had been eliminated from the equation. The Ivy League, a well-established and highly professional group, were hired as back-up singers and did their job brilliantly, but Tom remembers the problems involved in getting the end-product into a form he was happy with: 'We just couldn't seem to get the sound right, despite trying various permutations of instruments and balance. Then, after a lot of frustration, Peter Sullivan had the brainwave of adding brass. I wasn't sure – I didn't think the kids would go for a brassy sound at a time when most records were by all-guitar outfits, but I liked the results.'

The recording complete, more frustration ensued, with Decca rescheduling the release date several times: 'The final month of 1964 was the blackest time,' according to Jo Mills. 'We had run out of money and suggested that the lads

'When I saw my name on top of the charts in the Sunday papers, I thought: "Oh, thank God. This is it. This is the start." I've never really had a feeling like that since.'

'We were in a pub in Bradford, having a few beers, when the guy came in to load the jukebox with new records. People began putting on our record and talking about who this new singer named Tom Jones might be. The barmaid pointed me out and said, "That's him over there!" I was embarrassed but very happy.'

spend Christmas back home in Wales as we simply had no more funds with which to pay them their £1 a day.'

The folks back home gave the record the thumbs-up when they heard the test pressings. So did influential Radio Luxembourg disc jockey Alan Freeman, who playlisted it immediately upon its release in January 1965: 'I can't remember when I ever played a new record on air with a greater sense of recognizing a pop landmark,' he later commented.

Other disc jockeys were playing it, too, and a debut television appearance on BBC's *Top Gear* pop show coincided with

'I would like to go to America but only if it made me bigger. I am satisfied with this country and I don't want to be overexposed because I want singing to be my life.'

Gordon Mills's guidance) knew exactly how far to go, the tempestuous Proby defied authority – in the shape of theatre managements and local councils – by ignoring their warnings and going way beyond the limits with his raunchy act, the climax of which was his trousers splitting.

RIGHT: When American P.J. Proby and Tom eventually appeared on stage together, it was Tom who won over the audience and the critics. One split pair of trousers too many eventually brought Proby's career to an early end.

the good news that the record had entered the national charts at a creditable Number 21. Strong airplay meant live bookings around the country, and the snowball gathered momentum. Within a few weeks 'It's Not Unusual' had vaulted up the charts to reach Number One on the most appropriate of dates for a Welsh artist – March 1, St David's Day. In just four weeks the record had sold more than 800,000 copies.

'Not surprisingly, comparisons were soon being made between Tom and the British-domiciled American artist P.J. Proby. Both showed a strong Elvis Presley influence in their hip-thrusting and decidedly sensual stage personas; they dressed alike, with frilly shirts and tight trousers; both had their hair tied back in a ribbon; and both had big, resonant voices. But, while Tom (with

RIGHT: Tom's first hit —
a Number One with 'It's
Not Unusual', came
appropriately on St.
David's Day, 1 March
1965.

When they finally appeared on the same show — a charity event at Wembley's Empire Pool in March 1965 — Tom's sheer charisma won out against Proby's excess. And, when Proby was booted off Cilla Black's nationwide tour for splitting his trousers one time too many, it was Tom Jones who was brought in as a replacement, even managing to win over the P.J. fans who had lined the front row of the stalls with 'We want P.J.' banners.

The astute Gordon Mills realized that image was an all-important element if the bandwagon was to be kept rolling. For this reason, at a time when so many young girls made a habit of 'falling in love' with their favourite stars, he decreed that Tom's marriage — and certainly his fatherhood — should remain distinctly out of the picture.

Of course, it couldn't stay that way for long. When the truth did come out, Linda said happily: 'I'm glad that's over. I found it very hard to keep the secret, and so did everyone who knows us.'

AMERICA CALLING

'When I went to America, some of the great black Soul singers told me they'd never heard a white man sound so much like one of their own before. I was surprised and flattered. If they believe that I sound like them, well, I think that's great.'

FACING PAGE: Tom Jones looking the part for his projected role as The Matador.

It would be something of an exaggeration to say there was dancing in the streets of Pontypridd the night 'It's Not Unusual' hit the Number One spot, but certainly there was a fair deal of revelry. Tom Woodward Sr observed: 'When I got to the surface after a shift under ground, my mates gave me the news – and showed me the Sunday papers to prove it. We went home and celebrated, with champagne and whisky and all the neighbours knocking on the door. It was quite a party.'

Soon Tom himself was back home. The Wheatsheaf pub was commandeered for the evening by family, friends and a host of reporters, although Tom's mother tried to keep her son's feet on the ground with the reminder: 'Listen, Tommy boy. You might be a big shot up in London but down in Pontypridd you wipe your shoes when you come in, you're good to your wife and you take your turn bringing in the coal.'

This wasn't to be a prolonged homecoming, though, for Tom was now setting his sights firmly on the potential riches available on the far side of the Atlantic. Gordon Mills was making up in sheer savvy for what he might have lacked in business experience. His phone

LEFT: Tom carries his own inimitable style into the Nineties with a return to black leather.

RIGHT: Sun out, top down – fast cars were just one of the joys of new-found stardom. At one stage, Tom, Engelbert Humperdinck and their mentor Gordon Mills bought indentical Rolls Royces.

was red-hot as he lined up deals for his protegé – including the invaluable Stateside exposure of five shows on the nationally syndicated and highly influential *Ed Sullivan Show*, which had already been used as a crucial springboard by the Beatles in their own conquest of America.

Within a month of their Number One British success, Jones and Mills were on a jet – the latter overcoming his lifelong fear of flying – for the first show, strategically timed to coincide with the American release of 'It's Not Unusual', on April 29, 1965

If P. J. Proby's outrageous sexuality had been too much for British producers, the Ed Sullivan people found even Tom Jones's more politely thrusting pelvis too radical for a nation which, while it had spawned rock'n'roll in the first place, had in the early days often seen people decrying it as 'the Devil's music'. The cameramen were instructed to show the exciting new British star only from the waist up, and Tom himself was warned that, if he went over the top, his act would be pulled from the show. Proby might have failed to heed the advice; Tom was too shrewd for that, and his appearances proved a great success.

Back from that whirlwind American visit, Tom, Gordon and their wives took a short holiday break in France, driving to the Riviera in Gordon's new Ford Consul. Then they returned to the pressing agenda of cementing the success which would put them in Rolls Royce territory – and which had already earned

ABOVE: Tom's house — he always wanted to live in the most luxurious style.

mansion in Shepperton and we were all sharing a modest semi in Hounslow. He had a Jaguar and we had a van. We had no idea how much he was earning, but it was a whole lot more than the £30 a week musicians' wages Gordon had put us on. And yet we'd all been through the dark days of Ladbroke Grove as one, and the promise then had been that we would all make the big time together. We didn't rock the boat though because, in those days, even £30 a week was considerably higher than the average working wage and we were having a great time, with parties and girls all the way.'

Mickey Gee — who, as the only one of the group able to read music, had been given the title Musical Director — agreed that there were considerable fringe benefits during that heady period, but that there were also downsides: 'We just used to drink as much as we could and score with one girl after another. As soon as Tom found success, we all became mere employees, though. Dave Cooper got the sack because he wasn't a very good musician [he was replaced by keyboard player Vic Cooper — no relation — from Johnny Kidd and the Pirates]. But then nor were any of

Tom enough money to buy that long-coveted E-type Jag as well as a quite substantial detached house in the pleasant Thameside London suburb of Shepperton, bought for the then-considerable price of £7000.

The Squires were enjoying some reflected glory, but not too much else. As Vernon Hopkins, the erstwhile leader of the group, put it: "Tom was in a big

RIGHT: *Tom at the time of the release of 'What's New Pussycat'. The single became a world-wide hit and cemented Tom's status as much more than a one-hit wonder.*

us, though Chris Slade, who was truly dreadful to start with, did take lessons and eventually became a great drummer. Vernon wasn't much of a musician either but it was his band, so he should have got something out of it. As Musical Director I didn't do too badly, I suppose, because Tom took me out to Bermuda but I gave up my chance to visit Los Angeles with him so that Linda could go instead, and that's how I missed getting to meet Elvis Presley. I really didn't like the way things were going and I left – there was supposed to be a showdown between all of us and Tom and Gordon, but the other lads backed down and left me out on a limb. The attitude was "take it or leave it", so I left it.'

The bland 'Once Upon A Time' proved a rather disappointing follow-up to 'It's Not Unusual', but Tom was back on song with 'With These Hands'. A bit later in 1964 – after a full-scale American tour as part of a coast-to-coast package put together by top television disc jockey Dick Clark, then the most influential man in American pop music – and visits to other foreign lands, 'What's New Pussycat?' was released to tie in with the movie of the same title, in

LEFT: A slightly different publicity shot of Tom, out in the wilds of America.

which it was showcased. It provided Tom with yet another international mega-hit – and saw him swapping Woodbine cigarettes and pints of beer for cigars and champagne as he rapidly sharpened up his image.

If his stage act still harked back to the rock'n'roll gyrations of Elvis Presley, Soul fans recognized a strong Chuck Jackson flavour to his vocal stylings. Indeed, on first hearing the voice, Black America thought Tom was one of their own. Tom had got to know the great Soul singer Dionne Warwick when she had been in London earlier that year, and now it was her turn to play host. During his American tour she took him to the Apollo Theatre, the veritable temple of Black American music, in deepest Harlem. Top of the bill that night was none other than Chuck Jackson. 'Would you come on stage with me for my finale?' said Chuck. 'When I tell them who you are you'll have no problems.'

Tom told reporters later: 'Chuck did a sensational show, then introduced Dionne Warwick and the Shirelles girlie group, each to tremendous applause. But when he said, "Please welcome a soul brother from England, Tom Jones," and I stepped out on stage there was deathly silence as they saw I was white, not black. He passed me the microphone, I belted into "What'd I Say" and brought the house down.'

Rock'n'roller he might have been at heart, but it was obvious that Tom's career was going in the direction of big production numbers. *Melody Maker* pondered over whether he was in danger of becoming a 'square'. 'It's true that doing these ballads might be giving me a bit of a square image with the fans,' Tom confessed. 'What I'd really like to release is a big Blues or R&B number, just to show everyone I can do it, but my manager points out the snags to me and I start thinking maybe he is right and I should stick to the kind of stuff I've been doing. I realize I am becoming known as a film-title song performer and now I am considering going into movies myself. I've had offers from Hollywood, but I want to make my film debut here in Britain. I was away from home for more than three months in the summer and it scared me. I will not be going away for that long again. My future is in Britain – it's more stable here. So much of the business in America is false.'

One thing Tom really did enjoy about America, however, was the chance to

'I'm not fussy about recording in America.
I expected American musicians to all be
fantastic, but in fact I think ours are better.'

There's nothing I'd like better than to be able to sit down with my mates in my local, just have a drink and play cards, but that's all in the past. If I went to the same pub now, they'd either think "Who's that Flash Harry throwing his money around?" or, if I didn't buy everyone a pint, call me a skinflint.'

FACING PAGE: Despite his globe-trotting life style Tom Jones still has a great affection for his country and his place of birth.

LEFT: The ultimate sidewalk salute for the Brit who took Las Vegas and L. A. by storm.

meet so many of his idols: 'I like just to meet them and to talk to them – fellows like Solomon Burke, Arthur Prysock, Ben E. King and Chuck Jackson. I've met them all and I've enjoyed some of them giving me autographed copies of their records. It's true, I guess, that most of the singers I talk about are coloured. Well, that's the way it is for me. In most cases they are the best singers. You can't touch them.'

By May 1966, while recovering from the removal of his tonsils – 'Since the operation, I find my voice is standing up to the singing much better than before,

which is a relief' – Tom was beginning to feel a bit more enthusiastic about the prospect of returning to America, this time for a month in Las Vegas in October. 'I follow Tony Bennett and Andy Williams into this new club called Caesar's Palace. I can't take my backing group with me because of union difficulties, so I'll be forming a backing band out there, but I will have my drummer, Chris Slade, along with me, because he knows the tempos of my songs. I must admit I'm looking forward to it.'

And well he might for, though in the event it didn't take place until early the following year and the venue was changed, this was to prove the visit that

would alter the entire shape of Tom Jones's career, transforming him from a pop hitmaker into one of the biggest names in show business.

In the meantime, he'd also altered his public none-too-complimentary attitude towards American musicians. As 'Green, Green Grass of Home', released in 1966 and destined to be arguably the finest and certainly the most successful record of his career – he had discovered the song on an old Jerry Lee Lewis album rocketed straight to the top, Tom sensationally revealed that he was considering an offer to join the Tamla Motown recording stable in Detroit as soon as his current Decca contract expired. 'I've had a great offer from Tamla Motown and it is under discussion at the moment. The main reason that I haven't done a really Bluesy number so far as a single is that I can't get the proper sound in a British studio and I will not use a synthetic sound. If I stay with Decca, then we might go to Detroit and use Motown as an independent production facility – if we can get them to agree to that. The musicians they use in Detroit are really top men and I would like to record with them, possibly using Holland, Dozier and Holland as producers.'

This deal never reached fruition, leaving fans to wonder whether the magic of Motown could have taken Tom Jones to new heights of creativity or if the Detroit Sound would simply have swamped his innate individuality, just as it did with Chuck Jackson, the singer with whom his vocal technique had most in common.

'For me, 'Green, Green Grass of Home' was a warm song, very sincere, and I liked it very much. I'm glad it made such a big hit for me.'

While everyone pondered on the possibilities of Tom Jones as a Soul singer, with 'Green, Green Grass of Home' he had ventured with great success into the realms of Country music, drawing critical acclaim from the Nashville pundits – not to mention huge American sales. Of course, not everyone liked the record. *Melody Maker* referred to the hit as 'The song the hippies love to hate', adding, 'Not since Ken Dodd tickled his way to the top has a Number One produced

FACING PAGE: Thirteen hectic weeks in Las Vegas during 1967 netted Tom a cool $1 million.

such a barrage of spleen from the self-appointed arbiters of teenage taste.' Tom replied in his usual forthright fashion: 'It doesn't worry me because you get criticized in this business whatever you do. I found the song for myself, so at least it's proved that I can pick my own winners,

---

'We geared up for a new, more mature audience. Out went the blousy shirt and on came the tuxedo. What amazed me, though, was that grown women started going crazy, just like they were teenage girls again. Nothing like that had ever happened before.'

---

and it has ended a frustrating twelve-month absence from the charts for me. It's also shown that I can slow down a bit. I used to think that every single I made had to be a big song which I belted out. When I played my version of "Green, Green Grass" to Jerry Lee Lewis he said he was sure it would sell a million – and time has proved him right!' Indeed, it passed the million mark in

LEFT: The man, his smile – and a sense of mischief.

Britain alone, making it the only single to do so in 1966. The resultant gold disc was presented to Tom on stage during the *Sunday Night at the London Palladium* television show.

Said Tom, aware of his maturing audience: 'I don't cater for the teenage screamers any more. That's why I toured recently with the Ted Heath Big Band rather than a group. It was a polished show and the audience had to sit and listen – and they really enjoyed it.'

Things were certainly shaping up nicely, with the British music press reporting that Gordon Mills would be flying off to America to negotiate a possible deal whereby Elvis Presley's near-legendary manager, Colonel Tom Parker, would look after Tom's affairs over there. Parker had already commissioned a specially made film of Tom's *Palladium* appearance so he could study the act. Tom's publicist, Chris Hutchins, nevertheless denied there was any possibility of Parker supplanting Mills: 'He may have a piece of Tom Jones but he'll be acting as an adviser, giving Tom the benefit of his experience and building him up all over the States, the way he did with Elvis.' Everything augured well for the great Las Vegas adventure.

THE VEGAS HIGH ROLLER

'I think that London's Talk of the Town
is the finest cabaret room in the world. I
proved there that I could hold an audience
for a long show and that really gave me
confidence. I thought: "If I can do it here,
I can do it in New York or Las Vegas."
I'm ready for America.'

FACING PAGE: The ultimate Tom Jones experience — live and kicking!

VEGAS WAS CERTAINLY to prove kind to Tom Jones but, as Stafford Hildred and David Gritten pointed out in their biography, it wasn't a one-sided affair: Tom certainly did a whole lot for Vegas.

'I could have gone to Vegas earlier and played the lounges, but it's hard to break out of that and then get into the big rooms. If you are going into Vegas then you have to go in big and I decided I wanted the main-room spot in the best place in town.'

As 1967 drew to a close, he was looking forward to his forthcoming extended stint in the world's gambling capital. *New Musical Express* discussed the matter with him: 'Tom Jones, despite a heavy head cold, looked like a man with a million dollars. He doesn't have it yet but he soon will have. For 13 weeks' work in Las Vegas next year he'll pick up the tabs on a cool million dollars. How does it feel to be worth 350,000 pounds for three months' work?' Tom responded: 'It feels great, really great but, in truth, the offer means more to me than the money itself. It shows that they have real faith in me as an artist.'

The report continued: 'Tom will use the skeleton of his act at the Talk of the Town earlier this year as the basis for his appearances in Las Vegas and at the Copacabana in New York. On to this he'll graft new songs and his hits.'

Rather than playing the Las Vegas lounges and hoping to work their way up, Tom and Gordon had been advised – good advice, which they took – to hold out until they were offered a main-room slot. What Tom landed, the Flamingo, was not the biggest venue in town but, thanks to him, it soon became the hottest. In point of fact, the Flamingo was then a rather faded, jaded place and indeed was not even trading when – while awaiting the opening of their new international property – the management decided to headline Tom Jones in a bid to put the casino back on the map (or the Flamingo into the pink, one might say).

The key was promotion man Nick Naff, a high-pressure operator who knew all about how to hype nothing much

LEFT: Wearing an outfit which could have been drawn from the Temptations' wardrobe, Tom brought the soulfulness of black music to what was, and is, essentially pop material.

into something very special – and in Tom's case he was working with superior raw material. Naff certainly went the extra mile in his efforts to create 'Tom Jones Fever' – a phrase which he created and put to use on plenty of promotional material. He even went so far as to put a bottle of 'Tom Jones Fever Pills' on each table at the venue and had an ambulance standing at the door in case anyone was overcome!

It helped that the Flamingo was a relatively small showroom with just 500 capacity – meaning that only 1000 fans could get in to see the twice-nightly show. Tom's series there was a perfect example of the old show-business maxim that it creates more impact to turn away business from a small venue than to struggle to fill a big one.

By chance, Tom's arrival in town coincided with the staging of a show based on the movie *Tom Jones* (1963). This show was running at a room further down the Strip. However useful it might have been to him at the start, the confusion between the two shows did not last long; the lines queuing to see the singer got longer and longer as Naff's 'Fever' epidemic spread to become eventually something that approached mass

LEFT: Raw sexuality has long been Tom's calling card. 'Tom Jones Fever' was fully exploited by his Las Vegas promoter, Nick Naff.

hysteria. 'Tom, Toast of Vegas' was the headline to a piece by British pop writer Alan Walsh, reporting that Tom reckoned it was his 'most exciting opening since the Talk of the Town'. Most of the big stars then appearing in Vegas had shows which meant they were on stage at the same time as Tom, but the great jazz orchestra leader Duke Ellington went to the opening night, and Walsh revealed that the Welsh wizard would be staging a special show for the celebrities at a time when they could attend: 'And it seems that one of the stars in the audience will be Frank Sinatra, who is taking an interest in Tom's career.'

Elvis Presley, whose own big Las Vegas comeback was just getting under way, was another visitor: 'It was much different', Nick Naff remembers, 'from their previous meeting in Hollywood back in 1965. That time, Tom had been decidedly star-struck as he met his hero. This time, it was Elvis who came to see *him*. Elvis never emulated anyone, but I know he picked up some ideas from Tom's show at the Flamingo and they showed up in his own Vegas show later on. Tom had a highly sensual approach, playing straight to the ladies. He practically thrust his pelvis into their faces and, young or old, they loved it and went wild.'

When Tom's show later moved up to the three-times-bigger International and then on to Caesar's Palace, Elvis was a regular member of the audience. Vernon Hopkins recalls: 'The first time it happened at Caesar's, I was playing the slot machines between shows when I glanced round and then did a doubletake.

'I think that sex is more open these days, not that people necessarily indulge more. Even when skirts were down to their ankles, girls used to lift them from time to time.'

There was Elvis with Priscilla. I told Tom and he said: "God, we better do a great show tonight."'

American music writer Ren Grevatt enthused about what he saw when he caught a Tom Jones show in New York: 'Women screamed, stomped and went limp. Girls seemed to shudder with rapture . . . there was swinging Tom, doing the sort of things, pelvically speaking,

ABOVE: Relaxing in the pool at his Hollywood home. Tom was so popular by the Seventies, he could not even buy friends tickets for his own shows, because they were sold out.

that few fans will probably ever see on the wide video screen.' Those sellout shows at New York's Copacabana night-spot broke the business record that Frank Sinatra had set there back in the Fifties.

America was kind to Tom, and he responded by slipping comfortably into the American show-business lifestyle, staying up most of the night, rising late, working out, jogging, eating big steaks and drinking copious drafts of vintage champagne.

While he was hardly forgotten back home – his television appearances received guaranteed prime-time screening in Britain – Tom's stature in America was truly phenomenal. When ABC taped six of his television shows in Los Angeles they received an unprecedented 30,000 requests for tickets, leading him at one point to remark: 'I wanted to get a ticket for one of my friends but there simply weren't any left.' Screened on both sides of the Atlantic, *The Tom Jones Show* was a big-budget extravaganza – funded by ATV's Lew Grade – that gave Tom a marvellous weekly showcase not only for his own talents but for a star-studded coterie of guests, including many of the artists he had admired so long – like his all-time hero Jerry Lee Lewis – and such mega-acts as Perry Como, Cleo Laine, Johnny Cash, the Bee Gees, the Moody Blues and even Janis Joplin.

Never one to do things in half measures, Grade smoked massive cigars that even Tom might have baulked at tackling, and was an impresario who believed that bigger is always better. Confidently expecting returns of more than £20 million for American sales alone, he offered Tom a contract worth a staggering £9 million and proudly predicted that the series – set to run over three years, with no fewer than 80 shows – would make Tom Jones indisputably 'the greatest singer in the world'.

The show's production manager, Billy Glaze, remembers the series fondly: 'We had the very biggest acts but they never topped Tom. By then he was a real sex symbol, but they made him do ballads, as well as all that raunchy stuff which had the women at his shows in Vegas throwing their underwear on to the stage. Tom was totally professional and a fast learner . . . The most impressive thing about him was his effect on women. They really did throw themselves at him. The whole thing about him was sex. It was his image, his way of life, everything.'

Tom's affairs were legendary, and his behaviour was often as bawdy as that of the fictional Tom Jones from whom he had taken his name. His liaison with the Supremes singer Mary Wilson nearly broke up his marriage, and he had shorter (or just short) relationships with a number of his co-stars as well as

RIGHT: With dancers in cat-suits and an orchestra in the wings, Tom always gives his audiences the biggest show he can muster.

'Continental audiences are different from those in Britain and America. They listen in silence while I am singing. Then, at the end, it's great . . . it's like an explosion!'

with numerous fans and groupies. He was a sex symbol who really believed in living the part – and by all accounts he still does.

While Tom Jones was busy wowing the fans and having a good time, behind the scenes Gordon Mills was taking care of business, extending his stable to include not only his old friend Gerry Dorsey – now metamorphosed into Englebert Humperdinck – but, later, the vastly different Gilbert O'Sullivan, the latter managing to attract Gordon's attention by camping out in reception every day until the ever-busy entrepreneur granted him an audition.

'The reaction was fantastic every night, which knocked me out because Las Vegas audiences are notoriously blasé.'

The money accruing from Tom's stage and television work not only funded his ever more lavish lifestyle but also allowed the family to move home first from Shepperton to Sunbury-on-Thames and then to a vast mansion of a house, Tor Point, located on the exclusive St George's Hill estate in nearby Weybridge. The property in Shepperton went to his parents as a present, along with a gleaming white Ford Granada so they could travel back to Wales whenever they wanted. Tom Woodward Sr was 56 years old before he learned to drive: 'He enjoyed it, so I encouraged him to drive my cars too,' said Tom, who by now ran the Rolls Royce and Mercedes Benz models appropriate to a show-business star of his stature.

Though his stage work in America took most of his attention during 1968, Tom did not neglect recording. Les Reed, who had co-penned 'It's Not Unusual' with Gordon Mills, gave Tom another hit in the form of 'I'm Coming Home'. Then came that massive success – the anthem of a man's revenge against a faithless lover – 'Delilah'. The irony of Tom's consistent faithlessness to Linda was somehow overlooked.

By 1969 Tom's career was at its zenith. He earned huge fees for a 41-city American tour, and by the time it ended had no fewer than five albums in the

American charts. For the Squires, though, the end of the line had been reached. The February 8 issue of *Melody Maker* announced: 'A spokesman for the singer told *MM*: "The Squires have been with Tom right from the start but there were two reasons why they have now amicably parted. First, Tom will be spending most of the year making his television series and any tours he does now are with the Ted Heath Orchestra, so the group aren't going to be working with him for a long time. Secondly, for some time now the group has wanted to try and make it on their own." The Squires are making a bid for the Pop 30 themselves — with a record produced by Tom's manager, Gordon Mills. It is a cover version of Joe South's American hit, "Games People Play", rush-released tomorrow.'

The truth was that this single release — a cheapo production — was a sop. The Squires were being unceremoniously dumped. The title of the record could be seen as an ironic comment on what was really going down.

Tom appeared at the Royal Variety Show for the second time, this time as headline act, and took it as a joke when Prince Philip asked him. 'What do you

ABOVE: Tom enjoying happy times with his son, Mark, and daughter-in-law, Donna Mark succeeded Gordon Mills as Tom's manager.

gargle with   pebbles?' Tom was far from amused, though, when the press reported comments the Prince had made during a speech at a lunch for the Small Business Association the next day: 'Last night we went to the Royal Variety Performance. The last man to come on was Tom Jones . . . It is very difficult to see how it is possible to become immensely valuable by singing what I think are most hideous songs.' However

'Sexy? I don't think that I'm sexy. It's just the first time that I've ever done "Land of a Thousand Dances" on television.'

angry Tom was – he was extremely so – the astute Gordon Mills persuaded him to temper his reaction, though Tom couldn't hold back from pointing out to the press: 'I make a lot of money but I also pay a lot of taxes and I also give my services to charity, as at the Royal Variety Show.'

Aware of the backlash caused by his remarks, Prince Philip instructed Buckingham Palace officials to send Tom an apology. When asked what he thought of the Royal Family, Tom diplomatically replied to the newspapers: 'If the country can afford them I think the Royal Family is a good thing.' Finally, the potential antagonists got to meet at a Buckingham Palace cocktail party, following a World Wildlife Fund charity event, and man-to-man the record was set straightish: the Prince explained somewhat implausibly that what he had meant was that, if a singer could make a fortune, then business people ought to be capable of doing well too. Tom took the explanation in good grace.

Internationally Tom Jones was now an accepted member of the show-business aristocracy. The shows got bigger, more spectacular and better – Gordon Mills

RIGHT: The Tom Jones magic — wringing all the emotion out of a song's lyrics. Luxury hotels, limousines and a 1971 tour worth £2 million were part of the reward.

leased a Boeing 707 just to carry the vast entourage across the country on the 1971 American tour, which netted Tom a cool £2 million. 'There would be a fleet of limousines, luxury tour buses and rooms in the best hotels. I've never experienced anything like it,' remembers one of the backing singers. Simultaneously the piles of knickers and room-keys showered on Tom by his adoring female fans just grew and grew — more than 5000 room-keys were collected in one week in Las Vegas alone!

'Your voice is a part of you and you just have to take care of it. This is the only worry that I have — to keep fit enough to give full value to the people who pay good money to come to see me.'

IN THE GROOVE

'Without any fuss at all, Elvis and his wife came to the show and sat right down at the front. He told me later that it was watching me on stage in Vegas which gave him the urge to perform again.'

FACING PAGE: In the Nineties Tom Jones has enjoyed a deserved and huge renaissance, most especially when he teamed up with The Art of Noise for the storming cover of Prince's song 'Kiss'.

GORDON MILLS put his finger right on the button. 'Las Vegas', he said, 'has gone absolutely mad for Tom Jones. If ever Wales and Britain should be proud of anyone, then it's Tom Jones — because he's the biggest thing seen here in years.'

'When I moved to Weybridge, I was in a local garage getting petrol and forgot to take my Green Shield stamps. When I went back for them, a woman said: "You don't collect them, do you?" And I pointed to my Rolls Royce and said: "How do you think I got this, then?"'

The 'Jones Fever' Naff had created had proved a highly contagious and acute virus. At one show, a beautiful young woman, wearing a slinky white silk trouser suit, ran frenziedly across the table-tops in her bid to get to the man — scattering plates, glasses and other patrons before being restrained by one of Tom's minders. Another admirer's man-friend was so incensed by her obvious lust for the star that he went for Tom with a knife. Yet another fan embezzled more than $100,000 out of her employers so that she could fund her attendances at show after show.

Some male partners were happy with the effect: 'You've done more for my married life than I can tell you. When my wife sees you she gets so charged up that she's like a young woman again,' one grateful man wrote to the star.

Tom had his own theory as to why American women were going so overboard: 'It might be that the American woman is a bit suppressed. Maybe she can't normally let her hair down enough with artists like Perry Como or Andy Williams, but with me she can open up all the valves. Kids don't have such problems, but with the 20-to-40 age-bracket women there's a need for such an outlet.'

Fan clubs sprang up all over the place, and prospered, thanks to the encouragement of the dedicated Annie Toomaru, hired by Gordon Mills to coordinate the activities of such organizations worldwide. One English fan made her home a virtual shrine to Tom: besides collecting not only all of his records and video

RIGHT: *Music to his ears?*
Sax player Curtis Stigers
serenades Tom backstage.

tapes of all of his shows, she built up a phenomenal assemblage of well over 30,000 press clippings.

And so the bandwagon trundled on. At one point Tom and Gordon – and Englebert, too – were spending up to eight months at a time away from Britain, wowing audiences in North America, South America, Australia and throughout Europe. Though absence can make the heart grow fonder in terms of personal relationships, it doesn't help to make hit records. When artists are not on hand for PR tours and radio-station promotionals, the charts soon become unresponsive. Years later Tom said: 'The hits stopped in 1973, when I moved from Decca to EMI. We had hit on a formula with Peter Sullivan, my recording manager at Decca, but he went off and formed a public company with Beatles producer George Martin and suddenly became very expensive. Gordon said Peter had become too pricy. I tried to persuade him to keep the old team together but he reckoned we could make hits with other people. We kept trying things with different producers but that formula thing is like a puzzle, and when you lose parts of a puzzle you lose the whole thing.'

Despite his continuing triumphs as a live artist and television star, Tom lost his grip on the recording game. Though a steady trickle of releases came out over the years, the hits simply stopped happening. What did he care? MAM – the joint company set up by Gordon Mills, Tom and Engelbert Humperdinck – was making fortunes, his old records were still selling steadily, the date-sheet was full, the women were still fawning and the champagne was flowing by the bucketload. Between them, the trio had eight Rolls Royces and a company jet. They and their entourage stayed at the best hotels, owned homes that were more like palaces and had the world at their feet.

If the hits – or lack of them – stopped getting his name into the charts, the personal scandals certainly maintained Tom Jones's headline-news value: 'Their womanizing was legendary,' recalls music journalist Peter Kent, then with *Record Mirror*. 'They had the pick of the most beautiful women in the world but Tom didn't care whether his partner for the night was a beautiful starlet or a middle-aged matron. He loved them all . . . literally.'

It was a different setting and with different props, but this was essentially a more sophisticated version of the 'Jack the Lad' lifestyle that Tom had enjoyed during his youth back in the South Wales valleys. Just as had happened way back then, it often got him into trouble – no more so than when his publicist, Chris Hutchins, maybe sensing that for him the gravy train was about to stop, turned Judas and spilled the beans to a British tabloid, the *Daily Mirror*, in a sensational sequence of revelations about Tom Jones's excesses and orgies. In a series titled *The Family*, the vitriolic Hutchins described Tom as an ageing, uncouth, semi-literate womanizing slob and Gordon Mills as a ruthless, arrogant and greedy exploiter. It was strong stuff and it sold newspapers. If anything, though, it served to make Tom even more of a superstar.

Like Frank Sinatra and Elvis Presley before him, Tom Jones surrounded himself with an inner circle of minders, confidantes and party-sharers who could partake of the fun while he picked up the tab. His old friends from Pontypridd Chris Ellis and Dai Perry and Gordon Mills's fellow former bus conductor friend Rocky Seddon all had serious jobs to do within the 'Jones Boy Mafia', but

> *'Las Vegas is like home to me. The only trouble is, it's a bit like working down the coal mines of Wales . . . I rarely get to see the daylight!'*

once showtime had been and gone and their tasks had been fulfilled, they hung around and went into overtime, taking their reward in good food, fine wine and lots of women.

Back in 1974 the story went round that leggy Miss World winner Marji Wallace was sexually involved not only with racing driver Peter Reveson and soccer star George Best – both sex symbols in their own right – but with Tom Jones, whom she had met on the set of the BBC Television spectacular *Tom Jones on Happiness Island*. Allegedly, she kept score and, while Best rated a lowly three, Tom scored nine out of 10. Five years on, a book could have been filled several times over with such tales – some mythical, created by story-hungry journalists or spurned former friends, but most of them probably true. An example of the latter is the story of the child born to an American lover who won a paternity suit against the star following a court-ordered blood test.

'I'm not a frustrated actor, nothing like that. In fact, I've always looked on acting as hard work and now, after working on PLEASURE COVE, I know that's true.'

While he has tasted massive chart success, conquered the concert scene and become a major television star, one area of success has continued to elude Tom Jones – he has never made it into the big-time movies. Despite an ongoing succession of headline stories that he would appear in this or that blockbuster, and despite his having cut the soundtrack themes for *Thunderball* (1965) and *What's New Pussycat?* (1963), he has not appeared on the silver screen. The nearest he has got has been a role as a smuggler in the NBC television movie *Pleasure Cove* (1979). This movie was not a critical success, leading his cousin, Alan Woodward, to advise Tom: 'If I was you, I'd stick to singing!'

From Vegas Tom moved on at the end of the Seventies to the rival gambling resort of Atlantic City, across on the East Coast. Here, too, the menfolk gambled while their women swooned over Tom Jones. Colin Macfarlane expressed it perfectly in his biography of the star: 'He whipped the largely female audiences into a state of sexual frenzy. Before each show they would spend, spend, spend, to get charged up, and after each show they would spend, spend, spend again. Tom attracted the right sort of crowd – middle-aged, middle-class women who had terrific spending power and who brought their husbands along to the casino . . . Week in, week out, Tom earned himself the equivalent of a pools win.'

Fêted everywhere, Tom even got to spar – for fun – with his old chum Muhammad Ali, then in training for his title fight with Larry Holmes. Ali accidentally drew blood from Tom's mouth: 'Careful, I've got a thousand dollars' worth of capped teeth,' quipped the singer, who by this time had also undergone a series of nose jobs to undo the damage from the scraps he had endured as a teenage yobbo back in Wales.

Tom was quite open about his attitude to plastic surgery: 'I had to be honest about it because it's so apparent,' he told a *Melody Maker* reporter. 'People have seen early pictures of me and know that I had a busted nose. So I just tell 'em, "Yeah, I've had it fixed, and I'll have a face-lift when I need one, too. When the eyes get too much, the bags will get taken out!" Instead of buying another diamond ring, you get your looks fixed. It's just about trying to look better, you know, and there's nothing wrong with that.'

By now living permanently in California – though his wife Linda elected to remain back home in Britain – Tom still felt the need for strong family ties, adding son Mark to his entourage and frequently introducing his father to the stars. When Tom Woodward Sr died in 1981, at the age of 72, his son cancelled big-paying Vegas shows at Caesar's Palace, and it was reported that he wept for days.

Another death, five years later, had a profound effect on his career. Having recently broken for good with his long-suffering wife Jo, Gordon Mills was planning to marry Annie Toomaru but,

before he could do so, succumbed to cancer. One follower who remembers the old days vividly recalls Gordon's role: 'The group was very good fun. Tom was OK, but everyone else seemed to enjoy themselves even more – and Gordon was very much in control. I'm convinced that most of the party scene was Gordon living vicariously. On a personal level, being able to score with women, he was right up there with Tom.

RIGHT: Mature women might be the core of Tom's following – but it seems the kids like him too.

RIGHT: Harrods boss Mohammed Al-Fayed demonstrates the latest line in knickers — sure to be thrown at Tom in due course by adoring fans.

RIGHT: *Taking care of business — son and manager, Mark, with father and singer, Tom.*

He was bright, very bright, and had more charisma than any of them.'

Gordon's daughter Beverly added: 'Tom trusted Dad implicitly to do everything for him. They used to argue, sometimes long into the night, but not about anything to do with business. In that area, Dad was in charge, and that was that. No, they'd sit up till 6a.m. or whenever, arguing about politics or history.'

The aftermath of Gordon's death meant a major reshuffle of the Tom Jones organization, and in came Tom's son Mark as manager. Under a headline which simply bannered Tom's by now familiar nickname 'The Voice', writer Kris Kirk told *Melody Maker* readers: 'Fads may come and go but true quality never wanes. Tom Jones, the man with the voice and the electric hip thrust, aims to get back on *Top of the Pops* . . . Long before he became a noted recipient of middle-aged ladies' knickers, the 47-year-old man sitting opposite me, in black leather trousers and a tight black T-shirt from which bulge his newly developed biceps, was the best rock'n'roll voice Britain ever produced, Billy Fury included. Now he's back in London to promote

'*Moving from Wales to England in the beginning was a move. Moving to the States was just another move. Once I came out of Pontypridd everything else was foreign.*'

*'Knowing that I had this voice, ever since
I can remember — that's what has given me
the confidence.'*

RIGHT: Tom Jones the family man, with his grandson. The Nineties found him winning a younger audience once again.

Matador, a musical based on the life of the 1960s bullfighter icon El Cordobes, the lead role of which he'll probably play on the West End stage in the summer. It's a rags-to-riches story that could have been his own, says this roughhewn man from a Welsh mining community.'

Kevin Davies, one of the new breed of rock writers, was impressed by this throwback to an earlier generation and wrote in *New Musical Express*: 'Compared to Tom Jones, the average African elephant is a cowering shrew. The man is built like a brick shithouse. One expects him to have "GENTS" tattooed on one set of knuckles and "LADIES" on the other. Tom Jones is a big lad and concealed inside that unfrail frame is one of the most powerful voices known to nature, The Jones Voice. Even the bow ties and dress shirts Tom wears for his Vegas and Palladium performances cannot disguise that The Jones Voice is about to charge out of his throat and lay the audience to waste.'

And yes, at last, Tom was back in the charts with 'A Boy from Nowhere'. Delighted to be winning himself a younger audience once again, the now-grandfather was still one of the great sex

'I had Robert Goullet telling me: "You sing standards great. Forget this hairy stuff" and Wilson Pickett saying: "Christ, you're a blue-eyed Soul singer, the only white man who can sing Soul — so why are you singing this 'Fly Me to the Moon' crap when you could be singing 'Mustang Sally'?"'

'Touring? It's just like being patted on the back all the time. I love that thing of coming offstage after all the excitement and thinking, "Christ, you've done it again, Tom" — it's magic.'

icons of the age — any age. 'I never really think much about that, it just comes naturally,' mused Jones, adding, 'I liked going to ballrooms back in the Fifties, when I was a kid, and dancing, and I've just carried on doing that. On a crowded dancefloor nobody would notice but when you are up there on stage, singing and dancing, then you're isolated and then it looks, er, sexy.' Davies responded: 'The King of Rumpy Pumpy cops out! I was just singing and dancing, Your Honour, I never meant to corrupt the morals of a generation. All I can say is that, judging from the way Tom Jones dances, they must have been very broad-minded in Wales in the Fifties!'

In a review of Tom's show at the Hammersmith Odeon in 1989, Caroline Sullivan exploded a few myths: 'Myth 1: Tom Jones is a risible Las Vegas hack with no relevance to contemporary music. Wrong! If you have ever thrilled to pop music, you would have been Watusiing in the aisles during this gig. Myth 2: Tom Jones is a sexy dancer. Wrong! He doesn't so much dance as occasionally stop short to briefly rotate his pelvis in the lewdest manner possible then carries on singing. Myth 3: Tom Jones's audience is composed of our mothers. Wrong! There were more than a few hungry-eyed teenage lovelettes in the first few rows, all speculating on the source of the outlandish convexity at the front of his black 501s. Myth 4: The music press prefers Dinosaur Jr. Wrong! The massed journos in Row D were rocking out like mad and, on the goading of the girl next to me, I found myself standing at the foot of the stage, brandishing a hankie, with about 15 other women. Jones went from one to the next, blotting his sweating forehead with each person's offering (mostly knickers, for shame) and kissing each of them. Then it was my turn! He blotted, he kissed.'

And there, suddenly, was Tom Jones in the charts and back on *Top of the Pops* with 'Kiss', probably the kind of record he'd always wanted to make – a hard-grooving funk laden slab of sexuality owing not a little to James Brown and setting dancefloors alight in clubs up and down the country.

Cast the schmaltz aside, forget all those naff album tracks, here at last was the Tom Jones who had torn 'em up back in the wild rock'n'rolling days of the Welsh clubs. And a whole new generation was ready to throw its knickers.

RIGHT: Tom Jones is suave, sophisticated, and above all, the sexiest singer in the world today – according to his legions of fans the world over.